A TOUCH

"What does it feel like, Lena?" I asked, wanting to know what a father's touch was like. Or what anybody's touch was like, for that matter. How different was it from the way my mother had touched me years before?

I shook my head. Minutes ago I had been surprised by the softness of Lena's hand. How long had it been since I had touched someone, I wondered. Or someone had touched me?

"Like I'm the dirtiest, ugliest thing in the world," Lena said, wiping her cheeks with the back of her hand. "Like I'm not worth the water it takes to wash in the morning. Your father isn't like that. You would know. You would know by how sick you felt every time he touched you." Lena spit. "You'd know," she said again.

OTHER BOOKS BY JACQUELINE WOODSON

Behind You

The Dear One

The House You Pass on the Way

Hush

If You Come Softly

Lena

Locomotion

Miracle's Boys

I HADN'T MEANT
TO TELL YOU THIS

JACQUELINE WOODSON

speak
An Imprint of Penguin Group (USA) Inc.

SPEAK
Published by the Penguin Group
Penguin Group (USA) Inc.,
345 Hudson Street, New York, New York 10014, U.S.A.
Penguin Group (Canada), 90 Eglinton Avenue East, Suite 700, Toronto,
Ontario, Canada M4P 2Y3 (a division of Pearson Penguin Canada Inc.)
Penguin Books Ltd, 80 Strand, London WC2R 0RL, England
Penguin Ireland, 25 St Stephen's Green, Dublin 2, Ireland
(a division of Penguin Books Ltd)
Penguin Group (Australia), 250 Camberwell Road, Camberwell, Victoria 3124,
Australia (a division of Pearson Australia Group Pty Ltd)
Penguin Books India Pvt Ltd, 11 Community Centre, Panchsheel Park,
New Delhi - 110 017, India
Penguin Group (NZ), Cnr Airborne and Rosedale Roads, Albany, Auckland 1310,
New Zealand (a division of Pearson New Zealand Ltd)
Penguin Books (South Africa) (Pty) Ltd, 24 Sturdee Avenue,
Rosebank, Johannesburg 2196, South Africa

Registered Offices: Penguin Books Ltd, 80 Strand, London WC2R 0RL, England

First published in the United States of America by
Delacorte Books for Young Readers, 1994
Published by Speak, an imprint of Penguin Group (USA) Inc., 2006

1 3 5 7 9 10 8 6 4 2

Copyright © Jacqueline Woodson, 1994
All rights reserved

Speak ISBN 0-14-240555-8

Printed in the United States of America

For my family

Thanks again to
Sarah Schulman,
Teresa Calabrese,
Wendy Lamb,
and
Zoe Leonard

After a hundred years
Nobody knows the place,
Agony, that enacted there,
Motionless as peace.
—Emily Dickinson

There was always the Hocking River running a red mud trail through Chauncey, Ohio.

But Chauncey—pronounced "chancey"—wasn't always the place it is. Sometimes I feel like Alice in Wonderland whirling through the darkness until the other side of my world is illumined. And this is about Chauncey's other side, the white side, and that middle place where Lena and I met and came together, it seems, regardless. Maybe at this point none of this makes any sense. But it will. It seems like it was a long time ago that none of it made any sense to me.

When it rains, the Hocking rises up. Sometimes it floods. Once, a doll with one arm missing floated past me. Another time a mattress, then later that same day a bed frame, bobbed along in the water, struggling against the Hocking current. *Somewhere,* I thought, *someone's sleeping on the floor tonight.*

When we first moved here, my mother would tell the story of the way this town was: A long time ago this town was all white and church-mouse poor. My mother said that I wasn't even a thought then and that she and my father—ha!—they were probably just being thought of themselves. We're talking ages ago. The people living here then were living off of the state. "Welfare," my father always corrected her at this point. "The state," my mother emphasized. She always had nicer ways of saying things than my father, but my father considers himself more practical.

After my mother left, I became more practical too.

Chauncey used to be a coal-mining town. Miners dug straight down from here to West Virginia and probably circled around to see what they could dig up in Kentucky before ordinances bumped in and told them they couldn't dig anymore. By then most of the coal miners were coughing up soot and dying of black lung anyway, so weak and sick they had to sit back and take the government handouts. "This is what happens when people get broken," my mother warned. After a while I guess the government officials decided it was time for the people of Chauncey to get back to work and stop living off of wel——— . . . the state. Since all the coal was gone, the only work, really, was in Athens, which is a couple of miles south of here. The city of Athens built low-income houses and trailer parks in some abandoned area, then moved the Chauncey people there and put them to work in factories. Now Chauncey was a ghost town, save for the sound of the Hocking gurgling through it and the soft crunch of small animals moving through the leaves.

Soon after the last Chauncey person was moved, the government came in again and inspected the land. *We can sell this*, someone must have thought. This is where the blacks come in. People stopped referring to Chauncey as a poor-white town and started calling it a suburb of Athens, and soon people who had always wanted to live in the suburbs but either couldn't afford to or were being turned away from all-white communities started taking Sunday drives up to Chauncey. They measured the distance and decided Chauncey was commutable. They had picnics by the river. They took slow walks into the woods and picked the spot of land on which they'd build their homes. Slowly Chauncey was transformed into an all-black suburb. Stores moved here. Woolworth's, Save Way, Winn-Dixie. Randolph Park was erected, and a small pond was dug in the center of it. Chauncey Middle and Chauncey High were built.

No one questioned the past. Where did the children of

coal miners once play? Where did they go to school and shop before the new Chauncey was built? Who were they? What did they dream at night as they lay in bed on the other side of paper-thin walls that only served to amplify the sound of their fathers' coughing? How did they stay warm?

Years and years after the new Chauncey happened, the factory plan began to fail. Out of work, a lot of families went back to welfare. Some, having never really adjusted to city living, straggled back to Chauncey, expecting the town to be as they had left it. They found themselves in this in-between place, the only familiar thing being the river still gurgling past. Being survivors, these people settled in as best as they knew how. Because the houses they had once lived in were long gone, they erected shacks along the river or rented the storefront apartments that had somehow survived, and moved into crevices at the edge of town.

These people were older now, of course, with grown children and their children's children. These grandchildren are the white kids at Chauncey High, the tiny sprinkling of pale faces in town. They don't stay long, and it's rare you see black kids hanging out with them. Often they're gone before we know their names well enough to say "Hey" to them as we pass in the hallways. They keep to themselves, bring their lunches in grease-stained brown paper bags, eat huddled around the tables in the farthest corners of the cafeteria, their heads bowed in silence.

"Trash," my father interjected one morning when I asked my mother for maybe the hundredth time who the white kids were and why. "Trash," my father said, looking up from his paper.

"People," my mother corrected. "Poor white *people*."

chapter 1

My mother used to write me notes with smiling faces at the end of sentences. Sometimes she would write "Ha. Ha." if she thought something was particularly funny: "Your father and I are off for an 'exciting' night of gin rummy at the Martins'. Ha. Ha." My mother hated the Martins. She thought Terrace Martin was lewd. When my father's back was turned, Terrace would bite his bottom lip and stare at my mother's chest with his eyes half closed. Or he'd slowly purse his lips as though he wanted to give her a long kiss. Candice Martin, Terrace's wife, was a small woman—jittery, my mother told me. She said it was probably Terrace that made Candice so nervous. These were gossipy secrets my mother whispered to me in the dim hours of rainy nights while my father was in his den marking papers or out with his friends drinking. These secrets, my mother warned, were words that only mothers and daughters understood, words that shouldn't leave the four walls that surrounded us. But I shared some of her gossip with Sherry, and maybe Sherry shared it with someone else.

Some gossip I held on to. "Sometimes a person takes off, like maybe she's going to fly," my mother said once, her face dark and vague as the swamps behind Randolph Park. "You ever want to fly, Marie?"

Yes, of course I wanted to fly. I wanted to cast off, feel the ground drop slowly out from beneath me. "What is air, Mama?" I asked when I was five. Caressing the back of my neck with her hand, my mother waited a moment before she answered. "Air," she said, "is something there isn't enough of here."

chapter 2

I used to dream I was flying. I used to want to move through the air like a Para-Sail over Randolph Park. Maybe I dreamed on the baby swings. I remember how it felt to have my mother wiggle my fat baby legs into that safe place underneath the silver bar, sliding the bar down until I was secure, then moving behind me to push the silver back of the swing into the air, higher, higher, until maybe I began to believe that some tiny kid like me could sail away.

Last night I had a dream about Lena. She was taking me up in one of the big swings. There were other kids in swings around us, and the park was sunny and green.

Lena was standing above me, pumping her knees so that we swung higher than everyone else. I sat between her feet, smiling up at her, her pale, scarred knees touching my ears with each pump, air filling my stomach, making it dip.

"Not so high, Lena," I called up to her. "We shouldn't go so high." But Lena just kept pumping and smiling, singing, "S'cuse me while I kiss the sky."

"S'cuse me while I kiss the sky." Her voice gravelly and low as though she had smoked a million cigarettes in her thirteen-year-old lifetime. "S'cuse me while I kiss the sky," as though she thought she was Jimi Hendrix in the flesh banging on his guitar, his Afro blowing in the Woodstock wind. "S'cuse me while I kiss the sky," as though Jimi was screaming into Lena's lungs.

The swing swooped up past the trees surrounding the park, swooped up into the shards of bright sunlight streaming through the leaves. I felt my stomach flutter as the swing raced through the air, felt Lena's knees give one last pump against my ears. Then Lena's hands slipped away from the chain links, and I watched her sail away from me, in slow motion, over the fence surrounding the swings, over the pond and the gravel encircling it, up into the trees like a helium balloon. Up into the bright blue sky.

I dreamed I called to her, dreamed I reached for her and clasped a handful of air. Dreamed I was feeling an emptiness surround me. "Come back, Lena!" I screamed.

But Lena just pursed her lips toward the sky, her body growing tinier and tinier.

Then she was gone.

chapter **3**

I hadn't meant to tell you this. I swore to Lena I wouldn't. Even crossed my heart. She said, "Whatever you do, Marie, please don't tell nobody." When she said it, her eyes were sad, so sad, like a small dog that's been unfed for a long time. I crossed my heart then and touched her hand.

"I won't, Lena." We were huddled over a game of checkers in my room while Lena's little sister, Dion, sat in the corner pretending not to listen. Dion was singing to herself, a made-up song about horses and rainbows. Her voice was soft and high. "I won't," I said again, this time looking at Dion.

" 'Cause you're our friend, right, Marie?" Dion said. She had stopped singing and was now gnawing away at a cuticle.

"Of course I'm your friend," I said. Behind her, rain was

beating softly against the window. I turned back to Lena. In the gray daylight she looked older than thirteen. Maybe she looked forty. Maybe seventy-five. I stared down at the checkerboard. "I won't ever tell anybody."

Lena's eyes seemed to hold on to that sadness as though any minute she'd start crying and no one in the world, not even God, could stop the tears. She didn't cry, though. Behind the sadness in her eyes there was something—like a thin layer of steel. And no matter how hard you looked, you couldn't see past it. And no matter what you did, you couldn't melt that steel into tears.

I would have sworn on a million Bibles. I would have sworn on Christ's robe.

But that was a long time ago. This morning, when I woke up from that dream, I knew I would tell. It seemed like Lena was saying, *It's okay now, Marie. Go ahead and tell it. Then maybe someday other girls like you and me can fly through this stupid world without being afraid.*

So I should start at the beginning.

And tell the world.

chapter

It was the third day of school, and we were just starting to calm down from summer break when Lena walked into the classroom that Thursday morning. She stood at the front of the room while Ms. Cory introduced her, her head bowed, a composition notebook clutched to her chest. I scowled. Lena's clothes were strange. Her socks didn't match, and the heels of her shoes were worn down. To top it off, she was white. I put a book on the empty seat next to me, hoping Ms. Cory wouldn't notice that no one had been assigned that seat.

Sherry leaned forward and whispered into my ear. "White girl."

I nodded and prayed silently. *Please, Ms. Cory. Don't sit her next to me.*

"Marie," Ms. Cory was calling. "Raise your hand."

I sucked my teeth and reluctantly stuck my hand in the air.

"You can sit there for now, Lena." Ms. Cory smiled. "Marie will help you get acquainted."

Lena walked down the aisle slowly and smiled at me before sliding into her seat. I moved my book and didn't smile back.

She was taller than I was with dark brown hair cut short over her ears like a boy. My father would say she didn't look clean. Her hair was oily, and the shirt she was wearing had ring-around-the-collar. I glanced at her profile. She had perfect posture. Her nose was crooked, though, and seemed a little on the big side.

Ms. Cory was giving us a crash course on the civil rights movement. I half listened, having heard it a hundred times before from my father. He had marched on Washington. He had marched for desegregation and the whole nine yards. My father wasn't too keen on white people. But he had good reasons. Once, during a sit-in in Georgia, a white man hit him in the face with a stick. Another time he was arrested for being black in an all-white neighborhood in Athens. He has a hundred stories about how hard it is to be black in, as he calls it, a white man's world. My father said that when he was a kid, he thought people were just people no matter what color they were. But once he grew up, he said, he started seeing things in black and white.

Lena started working something beneath the desk, and when I looked down, I saw she had a package of cupcakes. She coughed loudly as she tore the plastic away, trying to cover up the sound. I leaned back a little in my chair to get a better look at her hands. Dirty.

"Want one?" she whispered, moving the cupcakes in my direction. My stomach growled.

"No," I said. "You're not supposed to eat in class."

Lena rolled her eyes and stuffed a whole cupcake into her mouth.

Sherry leaned forward. "That white girl thinks she's bad," she whispered, her breath hot against the back of my neck.

I nodded but didn't say anything.

Lena finished off the cupcakes and opened her beat-up composition notebook to a clean page and started copying the notes from the blackboard. She turned to me and whispered, "I'm Elena Cecilia Bright. Everybody calls me Lena."

Daddy would have said Lena was earnest. Her eyes were so serious when she said this, I wanted to laugh out loud.

"Who cares?" I said.

"Yeah," Sherry echoed behind me. "Who cares?"

Lena shrugged and went back to her notes. "I care. That's who."

Sherry and I had been friends for a long time. Our mothers had been friends. When my mother left, Sherry's mother, Thelma, came over to console my father and me. I didn't trust her. She must have known my mother's plans even though she swore up and down my mother had never said a word about leaving. Maybe Thelma lied to my mother too. Maybe she had told my mother it was okay to leave in the middle of her daughter and her husband's life.

Sherry is small with tiny feet and hands. Delicate. But she has a quick temper. She's pretty when she isn't angry. But when she does get mad, she isn't only unattractive, she's downright mean.

The morning passed us slowly. I kept stealing glances at Lena. There was something about her I couldn't get a hold of.

Though not a soul had invited her, Lena followed behind me and Sherry at lunchtime and even sat down at our table after she'd gotten her tray. Sherry and I exchanged looks but didn't say anything.

"Where'd you move from anyway?" Sherry demanded, shoving a spoonful of fruit salad into her mouth. She had spread a napkin across her lap and was glaring at Lena, who had left her napkin untouched.

Lena was thoughtful for a moment. She looked Sherry over, her eyes seeming to go soft with adoration. She stared longingly at Sherry's shirt, a blue polo with thin gray stripes.

If Lena had checked under the table, she would have noticed that everything about Sherry matched, right down to her black Converses. Lena's eyes flickered over to me for a moment as she stuffed half of her cheeseburger into her mouth. Sherry and I had gotten voted Best Dressed two years in a row, and we took our status seriously. I shook my napkin out and spread it on my lap. I was wearing a white T-shirt and jeans with black high-top boots that matched the black leather jacket I had finally shrugged off when I thought I was going to have to die of heat exposure for the sake of fashion.

Lena stopped eating and leaned on her hands, her elbows on the table. "I like your hair," she said to me.

My hair was short then, braided all over my head and tied with a headband.

I shrugged.

"I was *asking* you a question," Sherry said.

"What?" Lena rolled her eyes at Sherry, and my stomach fluttered. She should know better than to roll her eyes at Sherry.

"I *asked* where'd you come from?"

Lena gazed absently over the cafeteria, running her fingers through her hair. After a moment she turned back to Sherry, her eyes hard and dark. "From wherever. Chauncey ain't far from nowhere."

Chauncey ain't far from nowhere. I rolled the sentence

around in my head, liking the way it sounded. Liking the way Lena talked—like a black girl almost. For a second I wondered if she were light-skinned.

"Are you black?" I asked.

"Of course not," Sherry cut in. "She's whitetrash."

A muscle on the side of Lena's throat jumped, but her eyes didn't flicker. They were cold and flat now.

"You talk like a black girl," I said. The table had grown quiet, and I was groping for ways to fill the silence.

"I'm whitetrash," Lena said flatly, as though she had said this a hundred thousand times before or maybe heard it from a hundred thousand people. "Whitetrash," she said again, softer, as if the words were sinking in, finding a home somewhere inside of her.

Something melted then. It's hard to explain. I felt hot all of a sudden, and itchy. I felt like Sherry was sitting too close and Lena had drifted miles away. I wanted to punch something. I wanted to wrap my arms around myself and holler to the world, "Chauncey ain't far from nowhere." I wanted to wipe that broken look out of Lena's eyes.

chapter

Sixth-period bell rang, and the cafeteria came alive with kids rushing in every direction. Lena looked at me and sort of smiled.

"Walk me to English, Marie." Sherry got up and carried her tray over to the trash can, then came back to the table and collected her books.

I looked at Lena. She was staring off again, her composition book tucked under her arm.

"I have to show her around," I said, jerking my thumb toward Lena.

Sherry glared at me. "She can find her class. She's not retarded."

"Ms. Cory asked me to, Sherry. You heard her."

Sherry sucked her teeth. "You're just being an Uncle Tom."

I turned to Lena. "Are you ready?"

"Don't be an Uncle Tom," Sherry said, catching up to a group of black girls heading out of the cafeteria.

"Yeah, I'm ready." Lena picked up her tray with her free hand and followed me over to the trash can, glaring at Sherry's back. "I was born ready."

A long hall painted gray separates Chauncey Middle School from Chauncey High. Everyone eats in the same cafeteria, located on the ground floor of the high school. It had once been a gymnasium, but somehow, when Chauncey began to renovate, somebody high up decided to make it into a lunchroom. The middle-schoolers don't mix much with the highschoolers, and I sort of prefer it this way. My father said I came into the world nervous, and the high-schoolers didn't help this. Being tall and skinny and in the eighth grade didn't help anything either. Anyone who made eye contact with me would probably be able to see what a coward I was. Skittish, Daddy called it. "Like a mouse a light's been shined on."

Lena and I walked the halls silently, a few feet apart, while I studied her program card.

"Where do you live?" I asked. The late bell rang, but neither of us quickened our pace. I wasn't in any hurry to get to the right angles and isosceles triangles I knew were waiting for me in Geometry II.

"Over by the dump," Lena said. She trailed her hand along the wall, gazing at it as though she had never seen a wall before.

"That's kind of far. You take the school bus?"

Lena shrugged. "I guess. Could walk on a good day. Maybe hitch." She stuck her thumb out and smiled at me. One of her front teeth overlapped the other in a way that gave her kind of a nice smile.

"You could get killed hitching," I said, then realized how dumb it sounded.

"Could get killed standing still."

"This is you." I stopped in front of Lena's class and handed her the program card.

"We got any other classes together?" she asked.

I took her card again and studied it. "Ms. Cory for history and homeroom . . . lunch . . . science . . ." I looked at her and smiled. "That's last period. I'll see you then."

Lena looked relieved. She ran her hand over her shirt before reaching for the knob. "Thanks, Marie."

"Yeah," I said, turning away. "Whatever."

chapter

I had never questioned anybody's happiness before my mother left. Grown-ups were supposed to be happy. They had things. They had freedom and jobs, and if they were my parents, they had a daughter they had named Marie Victoria. But my mother hadn't been happy. Some nights, when my father was late coming home from work, I would hear her in the bathroom, crying . . . sobbing, gulping for air, turning the water on thinking I couldn't hear her grieving. When I asked her why she cried, she looked at me, surprised, then answered, "There is so much to cry about in this world."

When I was ten, I watched her walk away. It was raining the day she left, but she walked away with a suitcase in each hand, no umbrella, her back straight. She didn't look over her shoulder. She didn't wave good-bye. I stood with my father at the window, my head pressed against the glass. I watched her go, thinking she'd be back in an hour. That was two years ago. Postcards come with no return address. They come from all over the world—Paris, Lithuania, Spain, Bermuda. She draws pictures of herself on the cards—having meals in outdoor cafés, sitting alone by streams, buying oranges from sidewalk vendors. The sketches improve with each postcard. My father tells me that my mother always wanted to be an artist. I look at the pictures and wonder if she got her wish.

When her parents died, my mother inherited a lot of money—"More money than she'll ever need," my father says. They died in a car accident when I was six. My father tells me that there is money waiting for me too—when I am twenty-one. He says he wonders if I'll take off in my mother's footsteps. I promise him I won't. But this is a lie. My first stop will be Paris. I'll drink wine and eat bread and cheese at a sidewalk café. I'll look at the faces of the black women who pass, and search for my mother. When I find her, I'll send for my father, and even though it's years and years and years away, we'll be a family again.

chapter 7

Now my father was the one running every faucet so that the water gushed hard into the bathtub and sink to drown out his crying. I crept through the house listening, wanting to hear how people grieved when the absence they were hurting over wasn't caused by death. I wanted to learn how to grieve and how to walk through the world feeling whole when half of me had walked away. So I listened to my father and real- ized that you cry at night when you think no one is listening. You cry with the water running behind a closed door where you can wash your face and pat the red from your eyes. You cry hard and you cry alone.

Then one morning my father woke up and had a smile for

me, even though his eyes had lost something. He made the first hot breakfast we'd had in a year. He went into my room and picked out an outfit for me, even though I'd learned to dress myself during his absence. He pulled out a dusty black book and started calling women he once knew, asking them if they'd like to go see a movie or a play or maybe just have dinner somewhere. Some of them said yes, so he dug out that one nice outfit he'd bought a long time ago, gave himself a shave, found a babysitter for me, and left. But when he turned to wave and saw me with my head pressed against the window, that same window I had watched my mother walk away from, he swallowed, blinked back a new grief, and turned back for home.

"There's this new girl in our class," I said to Daddy that evening. We were sitting across from each other at the kitchen table, the newspaper spread out in front of our dinner. Daddy forked an artichoke heart into his mouth and continued staring at the paper.

"Is she nice?" he asked, not looking up. I had memorized every part and curve of Daddy's hairline a long time ago. Now, although he was still handsome by my standards, I was beginning to notice that he was losing his hair.

"I don't know. I guess. She's white."

"White?" Daddy looked up a second, his mouth a firm line across his face. A spray of black hairs sprouted above his top lip. Sherry once said men who are losing their hair usually grow mustaches and beards to create an optical illusion. "Must be trash."

"A person," I said, and heard an echoing of my mother's voice.

"Um-hmm . . . ," Daddy said, reading.

"Ms. Cory made me show her around."

Daddy looked up and smiled, shaking his head. "Donna's still trying to teach history?"

Daddy and Ms. Cory had gone to graduate school together. Daddy said he had never met anyone who *aspired* to teach middle-graders until he met Donna Cory. Daddy was teaching at Ohio University in Athens, tenure track.

He loosened his tie and pushed his chair away from the table. "Want to shoot some?"

"Okay."

I followed him out to the front yard, where he had erected a hoop above the garage door. Daddy grabbed the ball from beside the garbage cans, took a shot from the three-point line, and missed.

"Hit or miss," I said, taking a shot. It sailed in without touching the backboard or the rim.

"You gonna play this fall?" He scooped the ball from me, laying it up.

"I guess. Think there might be a new guard trying out, a girl who's pretty tall."

Daddy grinned. "Go up against Nelsonville with a tough guard and you girls got yourself a game."

Nelsonville Middle School had beaten us three years running. No girl on that team was shorter than five-eight.

Daddy dribbled the ball inside for a couple of minutes before I snatched it from him and scored.

"Man, girl! Where do you get it from?" he said, out of breath.

"Maybe you. Maybe someplace else," I teased. I shot the ball and missed. Lena flashed across my mind.

"Daddy . . . ," I began.

He took a shot. It bounced off the backboard and sat on the rim a second before falling in. "Yo!" he said, retrieving the ball and tossing it to me.

"I heard somebody say that whitetrash are the niggers of white people." I stopped dribbling the ball and looked at him. He was staring off down the block as though he were expecting somebody.

"I don't like you using that word—*niggers.*"

"How come it's okay to say *whitetrash*?"

Daddy put his hands on his waist and moved his lips to one side of his face. He was silent for a moment. "Neither one's okay," he said. "*Whitetrash* is just easier. Gives *us* someone to hate."

"*Hate* . . . ," I said.

"Not *hate,* maybe. It's not as strong as that." He was

thoughtful. After a moment he said, "Neither one's right, Marie. None of it's right. Just how the world is. White people hate us, and we go on hating them right back."

"I would think whitetrash is just as disenfranchised as black people. . . ."

"That one of Ms. Cory's words?" Daddy grinned. "Disenfranchised?"

I shrugged. "I guess."

He grabbed the ball from me, and I stood with my hands at my sides, watching him dribble.

"We're luckier than a lot of people." He stopped dribbling and looked at me. "I realized that after she left." My father's voice broke a little bit, but he ignored it. "I can't even stand the thought of her," I heard him say to Sherry's mother one day. But I knew this wasn't true. "I realized," my father continued, "if we can survive that and be whole, we can survive anything, and that makes us lucky. But we're still disenfranchised—we're black in this world, you're motherless, I'm a single parent . . . this list goes on."

"What if you're white without any money or white without a job? Seems like it would be the same."

"You thinking about that new girl?"

"Yeah," I said. "I guess. I never really talked to any of the white kids at Chauncey before. She's the first one. She's my age, I think."

Daddy tucked the ball under his arm. "I don't know if you

should think about her too much. They come here for a little while, then they're off to the next place. The rent's too high. The job they had didn't work out. Whatever. She came to school late, didn't she? Just started today?"

I nodded.

"She'll probably be gone by the middle of the year."

Daddy started shooting the ball again. I watched him. Something about Lena was staying with me, egging me on somehow.

chapter **8**

There used to be a commercial on television that got me all mixed up inside. It was about film or fast food or a long-distance call or something. I don't know. That's not the important part. But at one point this father took his daughter in his arms and gave her this big hug, and they both looked so happy and comfortable. That's the part that confused me. The commercial made it seem like they'd been doing this all their lives and nothing'd ever changed. I always thought that when you got to be a certain age—say, twelve—your father, because he was afraid, stopped touching you altogether, and that was just the way it was. Maybe your breasts were growing, or you'd grown quieter, or a couple of years before, your mother took off. Whatever the reason, your father decided no more hugs for you. Only, I used to think, what's wrong with hugging someone? Kissing your daughter's cheek? What's the danger of maybe, every once in a while, patting her on the shoulder and telling her she's okay? Somebody tell me.

chapter

Sometimes Lena walked like somebody broken. When I found myself behind her in the crowded hallway, I wanted to punch her back straight, to yank her head up, focus her eyes away from the floor. Other times she moved through the hallway like a steel wall, impenetrable and upright. Then I was a little bit afraid that she'd turn around, see me behind her, and explode.

I had seen my mother shake my daddy's hand off of her like it was a snake, snap back away from him as though his touch burned, then let go of spit and screams and send tears and snot flying. Screaming so loudly, I couldn't hear the words but felt them. My father's hands reaching into the air to calm her. Trembling dark hands. So much fear in our house then. The medicine chest filling up with antidepressants prescribed for her: Prozac. Desipramine. Phenelzine. Trimipramine. My father worried she would take too many or forget to take any. Afraid of the screaming. Afraid my mother would wake up one morning unable to inhale and begin choking for air.

Lena refused to click with the other white kids at school, and Sherry made sure the black kids stayed far away from her. Until I started walking with her, she walked the halls alone, always solemn and distant.

"Why do you stare at that girl like that?" Sherry asked, glaring in Lena's direction. Lena looked up and smiled her crooked smile. I felt my own lips curving up at the edges. We were sitting in the cafeteria. Lena sat at our table, a few seats away from the rest of us.

I shrugged, then thought better of it. Sherry had been getting on my nerves in the past few weeks, bossing everyone who looked in her direction. I hadn't known until that moment that I was sick and tired of her.

"Because I feel like it, Sherry. I stare because I feel like it. Is that a problem?"

Sherry looked at the other two girls sitting with us, then back at me. One of the girls, Chrystal, played ball with me in the winter. I watched her look from me to Sherry, then back again and smirk.

"You act like you want to kiss her butt," Sherry said, loud enough for Lena and everyone else within four tables to hear.

I swallowed, feeling my old fear of Sherry surface.

Sherry turned to Chrystal. "Don't it seem like she wants to kiss butt?"

Chrystal shrugged.

"I don't want to kiss anybody's butt. . . ."

"Except hers," Sherry said, jerking her head in Lena's direction.

I felt my lunch moving back up to my throat. Sherry and I had been friends a long time, and now I realized it was because I was too afraid to ever be anything else. Girls flocked around her, clinging to her every word. Not because what she said was so profound but because of the way she walked, dressed, wore her hair. Today it was in a ponytail, slicked back. Most times she wore it out, and the tiny brownish-gold coils framed her face. I twisted one of my braids around my finger, staring out at the cafeteria. A group of boys sat at the table next to ours, cruising us. I rolled my eyes. Sherry and Chrystal knew everything there was to know about flirting—how to ignore boys and keep them interested, how to walk in a way that made boys check them out, how to move their arms and hands and butts so that the boys continued to clamber for the tables closest to ours.

So many girls at Chauncey wanted to be like Sherry, myself included. If it hadn't been for Sherry, I wouldn't have been voted Best Dressed. I mimicked her style and added my own touches only when I realized I *could* dress myself and look halfway decent.

"I don't want to kiss anybody's butt," I said, realizing I had been kissing hers for years and years. I slammed my seat away from the table and rose, yanking my tray so hard, my milk turned over. "I especially don't want to kiss your sorry behind," I said as I walked away. Behind me I felt everybody's eyes, even Lena's, burning holes into my back.

"You are so tired," I heard Sherry say. "So very, very *s-t-a-l-e.*"

Then all of them were laughing, even Lena, her laughter low and hollow, rising above everyone else's as if she were trying her best to laugh the hardest.

chapter 10

"I wasn't laughing at you," Lena said, leaning in the doorway of the bathroom.

I busied myself with washing my hands, hoping she wouldn't see that I had been crying. "I don't give a damn who you were laughing at."

"She your best friend? Sherry? What's she to you?" Lena walked into the bathroom, hoisted herself up on the sink beside mine, and began swinging her feet. She was wearing running shoes that looked about a thousand years old.

I splashed water on my face, then searched for a paper towel. Both dispensers were empty, so I went into one of the stalls and pulled a long stream of toilet paper.

"She your best friend?" Lena called as if I were a mile away.

"I heard you the first time," I said, coming out of the stall again. "None of your business who she is. What were you laughing at, then? If you weren't laughing at me?"

Lena looked up at the fluorescent light and squinted. "It's nerves."

"What's nerves?"

She rolled her eyes. "My laughing. My daddy tells me Mama had it. When things went crazy a little bit, she'd start laughing. Nerves."

"Does she still do it?"

Lena glared at me. "How the hell am I supposed to know?"

"Because she's your mother. That's how."

"She's dead. My mama's dead. Breast cancer. Didn't even smoke and she died of cancer." Lena looked down at her own nonexistent chest. "Guess that ain't gonna be the way death takes me." She started biting her pinky finger, not looking at me. Not looking at anything, really.

"Sorry."

"Ain't your fault. You ain't got to be sorry."

The late bell rang, and Lena took a flattened cigarette from her back pocket, struck a matchstick against the wall, and lit it.

I looked around, nervous all of a sudden. Getting caught smoking was as good as murdering a teacher, by Chauncey's standards. Both meant immediate expulsion.

"It'll get you that way if you smoke," I said. "I got to go." I began gathering my books.

"I'll stop before it catches me. Your mama living?" Lena took a deep drag, squinting at me over the smoke.

"My mother took a walkabout," I said, liking the way it sounded.

Lena exhaled. "She take off?"

"Yeah. Took off."

Lena nodded knowingly. "Left you hanging like laundry on a line."

We stared at each other a moment. I waited for Lena to blink, but she didn't. She looked me over carefully, as if she were sizing me up, as if she were searching me for some kind of secret. I stared back, fascinated, not knowing why. Maybe it was the way she talked. Maybe it was those feet swinging back and forth like nothing in the world mattered but the cigarette dangling between her lips, sending a thin stream of smoke up toward the lights.

"I have to go," I said, heading for the door.

"Marie . . . ?"

I turned. "Yeah?"

Lena jumped down from the sink, clipped the lit end of her cigarette on the wall, and half-consciously fanned the smoke. She checked the cigarette and put it back in her pocket.

"Your daddy . . . is he . . . nice?"

I shrugged. "Far as fathers go, guess he's okay."

"Does he do things with you?"

I nodded. "Taught me to play basketball pretty good," I said. "Maybe he wanted a son."

Lena looked annoyed.

"You got your own room?"

I held the door for her. "Of course."

"You like him okay? Your daddy?"

"Yeah, I guess."

Lena clutched her notebook to her chest and stared at me as we walked, her brown eyes full of questions. I had never seen eyes that could change so, as though she held every single expression in the world in them. "Is he perfect, your daddy? The most perfect man that ever lived?"

I thought of the conversation I had had with Daddy on Lena's first day and shook my head. "He's not perfect. Who is? You live with your father?"

Lena nodded, looking away from me. "I got a sister too. She's eight."

"Is *he* perfect?"

We stopped in front of Lena's classroom. She peered in. We were a good fifteen minutes late. "He don't like many people," Lena said. "Calls this a nigger school. Say I'm a nigger lover 'cause I had this friend, you know. We was real tight, and she was a black girl. He don't really like mixing races. Sometimes I try to argue with him, tell him this is the nineties and all. But he say if God wanted us to mix, he would've made us all one color."

I smiled. "My daddy's not too keen on white people. He spreads the word *whitetrash* around pretty freely."

Lena winced, and I was sorry I had told her this.

"He was in the civil rights movement," I said. "Got beat up a little bit."

"I knew you was different that first day, Marie."

"Yeah?" I said, flattered.

Lena nodded. "You got a way." Lena smiled, and she was pretty, almost, in a sad-looking way.

Before my mother left, I heard her say, "The worst parts of my life are over," and now Lena's look reminded me of that line—like she had already lived a pretty hard life even though she wasn't old.

What is it like? I wanted to ask Lena, to know that you had lived a life like nobody else's. But maybe I was just imagining she was somebody she wasn't—the way I had once imagined Sherry to be a friend or believed my mother would always be around.

"What you thinking?" Lena asked.

"Just about . . . ," I said. "About how I better get my behind to class."

"That Sherry," Lena said, her hand on the doorknob. "She was your best friend, wasn't she? Then I came and messed stuff up."

"You didn't mess anything up."

"You love your daddy, Marie? More than anything?"

I nodded.

Lena looked away from me. "I wish . . . I wish I could love mine. Love him more than anything in the world."

"How come you can't?"

Lena looked at the floor. " 'Cause he loves me," she said softly. "He loves me too much."

"There's no such thing as too much love," I said.

Lena looked at me, her back pushing against the door. Behind her the class became silent, focused on her slow entrance.

"Nobody believes it when you tell them," she whispered. "Everybody says it's impossible."

I started heading down the hall and stopped halfway, feeling Lena watching me. I turned and looked at her, neither of us smiling. "That's because everybody in the world wants more love."

Lena shook her head. "Not everybody," she said, and disappeared into the classroom.

chapter **11**

Postcard from my mother. Amsterdam.

> When I took these things from the house:
> some tapes, some books, my winter clothes,
> I did not know that these would become the
> things I own.
>
> What little I own now.
>
> You take what you need when you need it.
> If you remember, maybe, as you've been taught,
> you will pack a little something extra

In case it rains. In case spring comes without warning to find you sitting in a warm drizzle in a wool coat

Sockless.

Love, Me

chapter **12**

My father swore he didn't hate my mother for leaving, but it was hard to believe him. She had only been gone two days when I walked into the living room and caught him ripping their wedding pictures from the photo album, crying and ripping, snot dripping from his nose. When a month passed with no letters or phone calls from her, he began packing the clothes she had left behind into heavy cardboard boxes, "Salvation Army" written on the side with a marker.

"Help me with this," he said when I walked into the bedroom that day.

We folded the clothes silently.

When I came across a dress or a pair of pants I remembered her wearing, I had to sit on the edge of the bed and swallow.

"No crying," my father said sharply, eyeing me there with the clothing laid across my lap like something too delicate to touch. "There's been enough crying in this house to last a lifetime."

"I'm not," I whispered.

"Where'd she go?" I asked as he put the last of my mother's things into a box and sealed it with masking tape. I had been wanting to ask this question, but each time I approached, something in his eyes said, *Don't come any closer.* Now I had to know and didn't care what his eyes were saying.

"Sometimes people have to go away," my father said slowly. "To live."

"But she was living, Daddy. She was living perfectly happy here."

My father took my head between his hands and pulled me against him. He wouldn't touch me again for a long, long time, but I didn't know that. If I had known, I would have hugged him harder and held on.

"Your mother's out walking," he said, "trying to find a place where she can feel . . . happy."

"How come?" I cried into my father's stomach. "How come we can't make her happy?"

He sniffed loudly. "Some people," he said again, "have to leave to live."

Two months after she left, my mother sent her first postcard. *I'm in Florida—The Keys,* she wrote. *From here maybe I'll go to Cuba. I always wanted to see Cuba, you know. I love you both so much. Diane.* My father and I sat at the kitchen table in silence, the postcard between us. He picked it up again, read it, turned it over to stare at the picture of palm trees, then set it back on the table. I did the same thing until we had both read the postcard at least twenty times. Florida. Cuba.

"Is she ever coming back?"

He shrugged.

"Did you make her go?" I asked, staring at the postcard. "Did you make Mama leave here?"

"She had to leave, Marie," he said.

"But she lives here, Daddy."

"She said . . . there isn't any air here." He frowned. "After Grandma and Grandpa died, she started getting scared that she'd die without having lived. Does that make sense?"

I shook my head. It didn't make any sense at all. She was living fine here . . . taking care of us and being a mother.

"It'll probably make sense to you before it does to me," Daddy said. "All I can say is Diane had to go away. She thought she was going to die here."

"What's going to happen to me?" I asked, scared all of a sudden.

A tear showed in the corner of his eye. "Nothing," he said. "I won't let anything happen to you."

I wanted him to hug me then, to hold me and let me cry. I wanted my mother.

"You'll grow up," my father said. "You'll live. I'll live. We'll both be all right."

"All right," I repeated. "We'll be all right."

But we were a little wrong. A different kind of family now, our house filling up quickly with my mother's absence.

Outside, I heard the soft thud of the newspaper hitting our porch. I put my head down on the table and swallowed, picturing my mother in an airplane flying off to Cuba. What would she see there? Would she find another little girl she could dress in the morning?

I remembered the first time she told me she was going to kill two birds with one stone. She filled the bathtub with water, then added Ivory Liquid so that bubbles fizzed against the side of the tub. Then she put me in the tub and rummaged through the hamper until she found a couple of slips and some stockings. "These need washing too," she said, laughing and draping the pantyhose over my head. I had laughed too, liking the feel of the stockings and satin slips swimming around me.

"Gone," I said into the cool Formica.

chapter **13**

I don't know how much it matters how Lena and I became friends. I felt like she had always been there for me, some-where, a soul mate, another girl floating through this world without a mother.

In the halls she always found me and snuck up without me noticing until she was right at my shoulder, her small brown head bobbing, indifferent as though it was the most natural thing in the world that she had turned up. At lunch she just sat down at our table, not saying much, but I knew by the way she cocked her head toward us as she ate that she was listening, waiting to be included, and hanging on to our every word in the meantime.

Three weeks after Lena arrived, Sherry pulled me aside in the hallway.

"You going to hang much with her, Marie?" she asked, motioning toward Lena, who was waiting for me a few feet away, shifting her weight from foot to foot as she stared off.

I shrugged. "Sometimes. She's okay once you kind of get to know her. . . ."

Sherry took a deep breath, tossed her hair, and exhaled. "Look at her, Marie. She's dirty. She doesn't dress well. She looks like a ragamuffin. I don't know what you see in her. I wouldn't hang out with somebody who looked like that if someone held a knife to my throat."

I looked. Lena *was* raggedy. Today her hair looked as though she had tried to wash it, but it was still kind of a mess over her head. She was wearing a man's button-down shirt with a couple of buttons missing and a pair of baggy jeans with no knees.

"She is raggedy," I said. Lena glanced over at us, then glanced away. "She doesn't have a mother, though, Sherry."

Sherry raised her eyebrows. Ninth-period late bell rang. School buses had begun lining up outside, but Lena had asked if she could walk me halfway home.

"You don't have a mother either," Sherry said. "And you don't look like that."

I nodded, mad at Lena all of a sudden. Sherry was

49

right. Nobody in their right mind should walk around that ragged.

"I'm not going to be hanging with her much," I said. "Probably just today and that's it. You know I don't really care for white people anyway." I looked over at Lena again. "Especially whitetrash."

Sherry looked satisfied. "I'll stop by later on. Going to Jack and Jill. We should probably study for that stupid history test."

I nodded again. When my mother was still around, I went to Jack and Jill stuff with her and Sherry and Sherry's mom. Just about every black kid in Chauncey was a member of Jack and Jill, an all-black social group. But it had been two years since I had gone. I couldn't stand the pitiful looks people gave me there. Also, your mother was supposed to be active. Sherry and I didn't talk about Jack and Jill much or anything that might lead to a discussion about my mother. But sometimes I wanted Sherry to ask about her. Sometimes I wanted to let somebody know what was going on in my head.

chapter **14**

"Why you so quiet?" Lena asked. We had been walking for about ten minutes. I lived a good mile from Chauncey and was sorry I had decided to walk instead of hopping on the school bus. It was hotter than any day in October should have been. Sweat dripped down the back of my neck, tickling the middle of my back.

I stopped walking and set my knapsack on the ground, then went to work peeling off my socks. The inside of my loafers were damp with sweat. I balled the socks up and stuffed them into my bag.

"Because it's hot and you're raggedy," I said, clenching my teeth. I wanted to hurt Lena for looking so poor. I wanted my words to stab into her.

She didn't flinch. "Yeah. So? What's that got to do with you not saying nothing to me?"

She pulled her shirt away from her and blew down into it.

I glared at her. "You don't even care. Look at yourself."

Lena stared straight ahead. "I know how I look. Like whitetrash. Ain't that what you call us? Ain't that what you call anybody white who ain't rich and beautiful? How you know I'm not out here making a political statement or something?"

"You still don't have to go around looking awful. How come you don't fix yourself up? If you're making a political statement, you'll probably get a better following if you sewed a button or two back on that shirt."

Lena began chewing her bottom lip, the vein in the side of her neck pulsing in and out. "Or I guess I should take some of my millions of dollars and go buy myself somethin' nice." She glanced at me. "Guess I should sashay down to the department store and buy myself some school clothes, maybe get my hair done while I'm at it."

"I'm not saying that, Lena. I know you probably don't have that kind of money. But how about throwing your clothes into a washing machine and running some shampoo through your hair—"

" 'Cause I cut it short so I wouldn't have to!" Lena nearly screamed. Her voice was hoarse now, as though any second she'd start crying.

"You still *have* to," I yelled back. "You always have to take care of yourself. That's the way this stupid life is. If you don't take care of yourself, people are gonna move out of your way—"

"I *want* them to. Everybody. Especially . . ." She was shaking. But when she started speaking again, her voice was quieter. " 'Cause I get out of the house fast as I can in the morning and take my little sister with me." She glared at me. "You don't know, do you, Marie? You can't figure it out?"

I grabbed Lena's hand. It was surprisingly soft. She seemed stunned for a moment. Then her face crumpled, and she started sobbing quietly, without any tears.

"I bet you can be in your house naked," she was whispering. "I bet you can lock your bathroom door. I bet you can stand in front of your mirror every morning and take a good long look at yourself without . . . without anything happening to you."

People passing gave us worried looks. A black woman stopped and asked me if everything was okay, staring skeptically at Lena. Embarrassed, I pulled Lena away from the middle of the sidewalk, up against the wall of Woolworth's, and tried to look casual.

I knew what Lena was getting at. I had read about stuff like this. But it couldn't happen to anybody I knew. It happened to sad, foreign girls in Third World countries. To girls living in crowded apartments. Or in the South. What was it

53

doing here, in Chauncey, Ohio? How could it happen to Lena, the girl I was walking home from school with? The girl who sat next to me in homeroom? Lena with her ragged clothes and crooked half smile. With her hard, sad eyes. Lena . . . my friend.

"Let's walk," I said firmly, pulling her by the wrist.

She wiped her nose with the back of her hand. "My daddy does things to me," she said.

"No, he doesn't. That doesn't happen. . . ." I dropped her hand. She was walking fine on her own now.

"It's true, Marie. Ever since Mama died. Sometimes . . ."

"I don't want to hear it, Lena!" I said, putting my hands over my ears. "You're probably lying. Nobody really does that kind of stuff. Not to their daughter."

"Yes, they do," Lena said weakly. "But it don't matter, right? 'Cause you can't do nothing about it if it's your father."

I could feel my tongue pressing hard against the back of my teeth. I wanted to hit her, hard, for lying to me and thinking she could get away with it. "You're a liar, Elena Cecilia Bright. A dirty liar. No father is like that. You just want attention."

Lena stopped walking and grabbed my arm so hard, it made my eyes water. A group of small boys walking past us giggled but kept walking. "Let go," I demanded, but Lena held tight.

"You don't know nothing," she said. "Your daddy never touches you like the way . . ."

I tried to imagine her father, unbuttoning her shirt, moving toward her like a lover. . . .

"No!" I screamed. "My daddy doesn't touch me at all. Ever!"

Lena let go of my arm. Tears were running down along the sides of her nose, but she ignored them. "I don't got a reason to lie. What would I want to lie for? If anything, I'd want it to be different. I'd want it to be . . . like your daddy."

"No, you wouldn't," I said. We had started walking again. I tried but couldn't remember the last time my father had touched me, even so much as to kiss me good night.

"Yes, I would, Marie. Just if he didn't look at me. If he made believe I wasn't even in the world, that would be better. You think I want *attention*? That's the last thing I want. I wish I was invisible."

I walked beside her silently, her words fading in and out. I was thinking about my own father. The first time I got my period, he asked Sherry's mother to come over and talk to me. She showed me how to use a pad and told me I could try a tampon but I'd probably have to wait a while before I was able to manipulate it. She told me everything I needed to know about my period, while Daddy waited in the kitchen, his head bent over a cup of coffee. I thought of how far away he stood from me most of the time, how his hand always touched the air beside my cheek. I didn't know if his hands were soft or callused, his lips on my cheek chapped or wet, his hugs light or soft.

"What does it feel like, Lena?" I asked, wanting to know what a father's touch was like. Or what anybody's touch was like, for that matter. How different was it from the way my mother had touched me years before?

I shook my head. Minutes ago I had been surprised by the softness of Lena's hand. How long had it been since I had touched someone? I wondered. Or someone had touched me?

"Like I'm the dirtiest, ugliest thing in the world," Lena said, wiping her cheeks with the back of her hand. "Like I'm not worth the water it takes to wash in the morning. Your father isn't like that. You would know. You would know by how sick you felt every time he touched you." Lena spit. "You'd know," she said again.

I stopped at the corner. "I turn here," I said.

Lena looked down the block. Trees lined it on either side. Pastel-colored houses were set back on smooth lawns. "I ain't lying, Marie," she said. "I don't never lie."

"I have to get home."

"Marie, don't tell nobody, okay?"

I shrugged. "Tell anyone what?"

"What I just told you."

"You didn't tell me anything, girl. Least nothing I believe."

"You think you wanna be my friend?" Lena asked. "You think maybe that could happen? I ain't had a good friend in a long time. Somebody I could talk to."

There was too much desperation in Lena's voice. "What makes you think you can talk to me? What makes you think I want to listen?"

Lena dug her hands deeper into her pockets, glanced at me, then back down at the ground. " 'Cause nobody can watch their mama walk away and stay mean."

"I never said she walked away. I said—"

"But she did, didn't she?"

Lena stared at me, waiting for an answer. When I didn't say anything, she continued. "When my mama died, I stopped hating. What's the use?" She took one of her hands out of her pockets and ran it through her hair. It looked as if she had just taken a pair of scissors to it. "You can hate all your life and people still gonna die and kill each other and build churches and pray to God and hurt their daughters and—"

"What's the point, Lena?" I asked. I hated to believe how right she was. Underneath it all, Lena was a lot like me.

She frowned, shaking her head. "Maybe there ain't no point, really. Maybe I just wanted to say that."

"And waste time?"

"Yeah," she said. "Keep you here a moment longer . . . wasting time."

We stared at each other. I wanted to grab Lena and shake all that sadness and steel out of her. I wanted to know everything about her right then; what had she been like as a little girl, what did she believe in, who did she love. I wanted to throw my arms around her and shout, "Welcome home." But we stood there silently.

"So you think we gonna be friends?"

"I doubt it," I said. "How come you want to be friends with a black girl, anyway? You should make friends with the white kids at Chauncey."

"Because of our mothers," Lena said. "There's stuff we can talk about." She bit her lip again and held it underneath her top teeth. "About what it's like. White, black—it shouldn't make no difference. We all just people here."

"But it does make a difference," I said.

"But why it got to?" I heard her say, almost under her breath but still loud enough for me to catch each word. Clear enough for each word to hang in the air a second before settling into my brain.

chapter **15**

I found myself thinking about her in the middle of the night, wondering where she was, if she was safe. At school I found myself growing anxious for the classes we shared. On weekends I walked past the dump to where the long-forgotten housing development Lena had once pointed out to me sat crumbling, and wondered which of the single-story houses with their cracked windows and peeling paint was hers. I found myself walking slowly, searching the faces of pale, unshaven men. Was one of them Lena's father?

Around the end of October, the weather turned cold. Reluctantly I packed away my fall clothes and pulled out my winter coat.

Saturday I left the house early, eager to be outside.

The wind was blowing so hard that my ears and the tips of my fingers hurt when I rounded the corner of Woolworth's, bumped into Lena, and landed with a thump on my backside. We stared wide-eyed at each other for a moment, then burst into laughter.

"Where you off to in such a hurry?" she asked, helping me up. I realized then that I had been heading to her neighborhood, out of habit, to watch the houses and the people going in and out and wait. For what, I wasn't sure.

"Who's that, Lena?" someone said, and I noticed a frail girl with long brown hair and Lena's nose.

"It's Marie, Dion. The girl at my school I been telling you about."

Dion glared at me, then stomped over to Lena. "You ain't tell me she was black."

Lena grabbed Dion's collar and shook her. "You be rude, I'll twist you like a dishcloth!" she hissed.

Dion's bottom lip quivered. She rubbed the spot where her collar had caught around her throat. "I was just *saying*," she whined.

I smiled and touched Dion's shoulder. "Hey."

"Hey yourself." Dion pouted.

"How come you haven't been in school, Lena?" It had been a week since I had seen her. She looked cleaner. Her clothes were still a mess, but her hair was starting to grow out. It fell softly over her eyebrows.

"Dion's been sick," Lena said.

"I got chills and fevers," Dion said. "I was puking like Niagara Falls."

I laughed. Dion's face seemed sweeter than Lena's, more trusting. But the minute she opened her mouth, you'd think she'd lived a thousand years. She had Lena's gravelly voice. I stared at them, wondering if their mother talked like this.

"You want to come have hot chocolate at my house?" I asked suddenly.

Dion looked up at Lena hopefully. "I guess." Lena shrugged. She pulled the coat Dion was wearing tighter around her neck and buttoned it up.

"Rock and roll," Dion said. "I'm about to freeze my skinny behind off walking out here."

Lena glanced over at Dion. "We're just out walking."

"It's too cold," I said.

"I know." Lena took Dion's hand. We walked a couple of minutes without saying anything. Dion was humming softly, kicking a rock as she walked. I stole a glance at Lena, and she smiled with one side of her mouth.

"Everything okay?" I asked.

Lena shook her head. "Okay as it's gonna be."

I turned into my yard and Lena looked around, wide-eyed.

"This is it," I said, unlocking the front door.

When we were inside, Dion made a little sound like she

was trying to keep from coughing. "This is your house?" she whispered.

I led them through the living room into the kitchen. My father liked to do carpentry in his spare time, and he had transformed our kitchen into something out of *House and Garden* magazine. I had helped him take up the wood floor and lay down gray slate. An oak island separated one half of the kitchen from the other, and copper pots hung on silver hooks from the ceiling above it. Daddy had knocked out the fourth wall of the kitchen and replaced it with sliding glass doors so that we could have a view of our garden while we cooked and ate.

Dion and Lena looked around.

"This is the most beautifulest house I ever saw," Dion said, hugging me. She climbed up on one of the stools surrounding the island and began twirling around.

"Don't do that," Lena said.

"It's okay," I said, pouring milk and cocoa into a boiler, then searching the refrigerator for whipped cream.

"Whip cream!" Dion yelled when I set it on the counter. "I love whip cream."

My father came in when we were taking our first gulps of cocoa.

"Someone have a party and not invite me?" he asked, his eyebrows raised.

I introduced them, and Dion and Lena stuttered hellos,

looking frightened. I felt my own heart beating in my chest, realizing this was the first time I had ever had white people over to our house.

"I asked them to come over for hot chocolate, Daddy," I said.

My father nodded. "Yeah," he said, taking an apple from the fruit dish and heading back out again. "Hot chocolate," he mumbled.

"He probably gonna tear your behind into twenty pieces," Dion warned, her eyes wide.

"Shut up, Dion," Lena said.

"Yeah, Dion," I said, getting up to pour more cocoa. "Shut up."

chapter

Postcard from my mother. South of France.

> In this world in this age maybe you will have
> *perfect moments*
> when you catch the way light grooves across ice
> Or a favorite song reminds you of onion rings
> eaten at a diner in Long Island
> Salt no ketchup
> Although you won't remember your waitress
> the color of her pen
> whether or not she wore a "Hello, My Name Is"
> tag above her heart.

You won't remember how the icy air
pierced the tops of your ears
How your eyes burned
as you stared up at the sun.
Below you a pond frozen over sighed heavily
then gave in, cracking a curved line around you
while skaters darted past, oblivious.

In this world in this age
maybe you will have an hour to grieve.

Love, Me

chapter **17**

"Can I come in for a minute?" my father asked, poking his head into my bedroom that evening.

I was sitting at my desk working on an English paper. Lena and Dion had been gone for hours.

"Yeah," I said, feeling my stomach flutter.

He sat on the edge of my bed and looked up at the Bobby Brown poster on my wall. In the poster Bobby is shirtless, his hand grabbing his crotch. My father shook his head.

"Those girls," he began.

I twirled my chair around and faced him. "That's Lena and her sister, Dion. Lena's the girl I was telling you about before."

My father nodded. "What happened to Sherry?" he asked.

I stared at my hands. "Sherry makes me sick sometimes. She's always trying to boss me around and stuff."

"I thought you two were buddies."

"We are, but she's so bossy sometimes." I looked up at him. "Like, take Lena . . ."

"The one who just left?"

I nodded. "Sherry's telling me that Lena's this and Lena's that. How come I can't decide who she is if I want to?"

My father tucked his tongue into the side of his mouth. He looked tired all of a sudden.

"Marie, I was never really one for telling you who you could and couldn't associate with . . ."

"I know . . ."

"But I don't like the looks of those girls. I don't like their clothes, their eyes—"

"They can't help it, Daddy. They don't have any money."

"There's something about them," he said.

"The color of their skin," I cut in.

"Yes," my father said. "There is that too. White people can walk back and forth through this world all they want, but we don't have to be friends with them."

"I *want* to be her friend, Daddy. Not because I feel like I *have* to. I like her."

"Do you *know* her, Marie? Do you know what the history of race is in this country?! Have you listened to anything I've told you over the years?"

"Of course I listened. But you're stuck in the sixties. This is the nineties. Things are changing."

My father sighed and started rubbing his temples. He looked around the room. There was a picture of my mother and me on the nightstand beside my bed. In it her eyes are bright, laughing into the camera. He scanned the picture, then let his eyes move on until they came to rest on me. "Where are you, Marie?"

I folded my arms. "Chauncey, Ohio."

Daddy nodded. "And who lives on either side of you right here in Chauncey?"

"Black people," I mumbled, having answered these questions a hundred times before.

"And do you know why that is?"

"Because we need to stick together," I recited. "Because sticking together is the only way that we as a people can survive."

"Does that make any sense whatsoever to you, Marie?" He leaned toward me, waiting.

"Yeah."

He sighed, shaking his head. "I just don't want to see my baby hurting," he said softly. "I don't want this girl to come into your life, call you nigger, and leave."

"I trust her, Daddy. She's different."

"Do you know anything about her family?"

I swallowed. "Her mother died."

My father's eyes seemed to melt a little. But just as quickly he stood and walked to the door.

"You're old enough to make your own decisions, Marie," he said, his hand on the doorknob. "Be careful, sweetheart."

"You know what Lena says, Daddy?"

"What?"

"She says we're all just people here."

A tiny crease formed between his eyebrows. "I'm glad she can still believe that."

chapter **18**

Postcard from my mother. Bali, Indonesia.

> If I dare to blink I'll miss this moment in my life.
> Callow desirous years on the edge
> dripping time not yet survived.
>
> I want to catch life, hold on, swing with it
> Before I am let go.
> Before I am old.
> Before I am too afraid
> to cast off ground for rope and air.
>
> Love, Me

Lena read the postcard, then handed it back to me without saying anything. We were sitting beside the pond in Randolph Park watching Dion slide back and forth across the ice in her sneakers. I shivered. Above us the sky was a mean gray. Maybe it was going to snow.

"The way she signs it?" Lena said. "*Love, Me*. It's like she's asking you to please love her. Do you still love her?"

I nodded, tucking my chin inside my coat. "She's my mother."

"That don't mean nothing." Lena picked up a rock and threw it at the frozen pond.

"Means I have to love her."

"No, it don't. Blood don't mean nothing."

"Yes, it does, Lena." We were sitting so close, our shoulders were touching. A few minutes passed before Lena laid her head on my shoulder. It felt warm and bony. I turned so I could sniff her hair. The smell was unfamiliar.

"Blood is like an accident," she whispered. "People think just 'cause somebody's your blood relative, you have to love them."

I turned the postcard and looked at the picture. It was of a group of little girls dressed up like genies, dancing in a circle.

"I don't love her because I have to," I said. "I love her because I know why she had to go away."

"Why?"

"She would have died."

71

Lena lifted her head and looked at me. "I didn't know she was sick."

I nodded. "She was. Sick and tired. That's what she always said."

Dion slid to the farthest end of the pond and twirled, then slid back over to our side. "I'm gonna get some skates one day," she said before sliding off again.

"Sometimes I get sick and tired," Lena said. "What's *callow desirous*?"

"My father says it means she wants something the way a little kid wants something—without question, just like, I don't know, really badly, I guess."

Lena frowned out at the pond. "Oh."

"Do you hate your mother for dying?"

Lena shrugged. "It wasn't her fault."

"Leaving wasn't my mother's fault. She just had to do it."

"Callow desirous."

"Yeah," I said, pulling Lena's head back on my shoulder. "Exactly."

chapter **19**

"What do you think about when you stare off?" I asked Lena a few weeks later.

We were sitting on my bed separated by a game of checkers. I linked my fingers with hers. Her hands were pale against my own dark skin. She stared, as fascinated as I was by the contrast.

We had dropped Dion off at the library. It was her favorite place in the world. She actually had a temper tantrum if we picked her up too early.

It had been five weeks since Lena's first visit to my house. Now she had become a regular presence. Grudgingly my father accepted it, until one night he came into my room to say good night and said, "Those friends of yours, Marie.

They're nice girls. Maybe they'll stay around awhile." I don't know what changed his mind, but I didn't dare question it. Maybe he saw how happy Lena and I were together. Maybe he was beginning to see other colors besides black and white. "I sure hope so," I said, closing my eyes. I thought of telling him then, of bolting upright and squealing the whole story. But I bit down on my tongue, hard enough to bring tears. What if he snatched me from Lena and made me swear to stay away from her? What if he thought Lena was a liar? It was too risky, I decided. Maybe it was selfish, but I didn't want to take any chances. If Lena and I couldn't be friends, I was sure I'd fall right down and die.

"I think about my life mostly," Lena said now, staring down at our hands. "I think about my mama. The way she died, you know. We ain't have no money and sometimes I think she must have known about the cancer. She must have felt the lump they said was in her breast. Once I heard my daddy talking. He said it was like mama's breast exploded or something because the cancer just took over inside. I heard that they can save you—doctors can—if they find out about it in time. She must've been hurting, my mama. Must have just been gritting her teeth and living with it 'cause we ain't have no money."

I swallowed, not knowing what to say. Was it selfish of me to be thinking of my own mother? To be wondering if she was hurting? The pain she felt living with me and Daddy every single day when she wanted to be doing something else—had it been like a cancer? Is that what Daddy meant when he said sometimes you have to go away to live?

"I think about what's gonna become of me and Dion without a mama, and Daddy like he is."

We had not talked about Lena's father since that time in front of Woolworth's. I felt itchy, like somebody was peeling my skin back and exposing everything underneath to air.

"Maybe someday me and Dion'll go on a walkabout, you know?" Lena smiled up at me. "Just take off and be gone."

"Where would you go?" I asked. Maybe I didn't believe her.

Lena shrugged. "I go places now," she said. "When my daddy's touching me, I take off, boom! and I'm gone. Thailand, Colorado, the Blue Ridge Mountains. I think of all the places I've heard of with beautiful names and try to imagine what they look like in real life . . . until it's over."

"How come you don't tell somebody, Lena?" I said. "How come you don't call the cops? Let's think of somebody we could tell! I could go with you—"

Lena glared at me. "So they can come and take us away? So they can put Dion in one place and me in another and I can go through the rest of my life without ever seeing her again?"

"Maybe it wouldn't happen like that."

"It already did, Marie. Right after Mama died, there was this lady who used to come around to see if everything was okay. She was a social worker, I guess. That's who I told. Just mentioned that he was wanting me to sleep in his bed all the time where Mama used to sleep, and she snatched us right out of there."

"Where?"

Lena sighed. "They took Dion to this family in Nelsonville, and I was staying with some people down near Kentucky. They was okay people, but we should've been together, and the woman was always coming around apologizing, talking about she couldn't do anything about it 'cause there wasn't enough families out there who wanted two girls at the same time."

"But now you're back together. Maybe it's different—"

"We ran away!" Lena's legs were shaking. She seemed disconnected, like her body was on its own, doing whatever it wanted. She took a deep breath and put her hands on her legs to still them. "I found out where Dion was and went to get her. I hitched and stole. We didn't have nowhere else to go, so we went back to Daddy. Ever since, he's been moving us every time somebody starts sniffing around."

I felt like I was watching a movie of somebody else's life. Reaching across the checkerboard, I touched Lena's wrist. She was real, warm and bony and real. My breath was coming quickly through my nose. I wanted to open my mouth and gulp air.

"Nobody can't do anything," Lena said. She looked down

at the checkerboard. "Whatever you do, Marie, please don't tell nobody."

"I won't," I whispered.

Outside, rain beat softly against my bedroom window. I watched it for a while, wondering why this world was so *stupid*. We were helpless, Lena and Dion and me. It was like someone gave us our dumb lives and said, "Sorry, this is the best we can do." I pulled my knees up to my chin and wrapped my arms around them. How come this stupid world couldn't just let us go through life being little girls? Why did people have to come along and mess things up for us?

"What's your daddy like, Lena?" I asked. "Do you still love him?"

I turned back to her and leaned so close, I could feel her breath against my forehead. Lena squeezed my finger.

"I got to love him," she said hoarsely.

"Why?"

Lena's head moved slightly against a rhythm only she could hear. "Because if I don't, that only leaves me and Dion. And what if somethin' happens to her? Then it's only me . . . stupid, whitetrash me."

"You're not stupid and you're *not* whitetrash. You're just you."

"Who's me?" Lena asked.

"Elena Cecilia Bright."

"Elena Cecilia Bright," she repeated softly. "Yeah."

We were silent. After a few minutes had passed, Lena said, "You get scared when somebody dies, you know? You start thinking the world's just gonna drop out from under you."

"Is that why you love him?" I asked.

Lena nodded. "Didn't you love your daddy harder after your mama left?"

"Yeah," I said.

"See? You hang on tight to the little bit you still got left . . . even though."

"Don't you get scared that maybe you'll get . . . pregnant?" I asked.

Lena bit her bottom lip. "He doesn't do that," she said.

I wanted to ask what he did and how. There were a million questions pressing against the back of my teeth. But Lena looked as though she had taken off. She looked hollow, vacant as sky, and I knew she had said all she was going to say about it.

Outside, thunder rumbled. I closed my eyes, not wanting to think about what else might be happening in the world, right here in Chauncey and far off too.

chapter **20**

We lost our first basketball game against Hocking 68–49. Although our coach swore it wasn't a wipeout, none of us believed her. I sat on the bench sweaty and drained but buzzing on having the high score of the game. The two new point guards didn't do much of anything, and the whole team seemed to be having a hard time hiding how disappointed we were in them.

At one point during the game I looked up and saw Lena and Dion sitting beside a pale older man who looked like he could have been their grandfather. My heart skipped. Hocking stole the ball from me and scored. Throughout the game I could hear Dion's hoarse voice screaming, "Go, Marie!"

"Was that your father?" I asked Lena after the game.

The gym was beginning to empty out. Groups of people ambled past us, slapping me on the backside, congratulating me, and casting questioning glances toward Lena. Dion stood at the other end of the gym, taking foul shots and missing.

"Yeah," Lena said. "He's waiting in the car. He likes basketball and sports and stuff. But he got mad at Dion for calling out to you."

"Pinched my ear good," Dion yelled across the gym. "We got a car, you know," she said as though she were daring me to say different. "We ain't so poor."

Bile seeped up to the front of my throat. I swallowed. "I'd like to kill him, Lena."

She shook her head. "Then what?"

I felt my nails pressing against the inside of my palms. What right did he have even stepping one foot into this gym? "I should've told somebody. Pointed him out."

Lena grabbed my hand, holding on to my fist. "You swore," she whispered. "Don't even threaten."

"You should kill him," I said, snatching my hand away. Tears had sprung into my eyes. "Next time take a knife, anything! Why do you let him?" I wanted to scream, punch a hole into something. "You must like it!"

Lena looked as though I had hit her. "Come on, Dion," she said, turning away from me. Dion ignored her and kept dribbling the ball.

I didn't feel sorry. Not one bit. They were freaks. The whole weird family. I hated them all. "That's it, isn't it, Lena? You like it." I had never hated someone so much in my life.

"Shut up!" Lena said. "You . . . you . . ."

"Are you gonna call me nigger now?" A part of me wanted her to so that I could hit her, for real. Hard.

Lena was crying. "Don't be hating *me*," she said. "It ain't about *me*!"

I hugged myself and closed my eyes. Behind my lids I saw him, old and pale and ugly. The ugliest man I had ever seen. I realized it *wasn't* about Lena. It was him I was mad at. But he was too old, too white, a man. There were a hundred reasons I couldn't get mad at him. No matter how much I wanted to.

"It ain't about *me*," Lena said again, shaking my shoulder. I opened my eyes. She looked beaten and old. Maybe she'd look exactly the same when she was forty. Or seventy-five.

"I know," I said softly, taking the hand on my shoulder between both of mine. I couldn't tell which of us was trembling.

"Don't go hating me for something that ain't my fault, Marie." Lena wiped her eyes.

I smiled. "Crybaby."

"You're a crybaby." Lena laughed.

We didn't say anything. Dion was kicking the ball against the bleachers, then running to retrieve it.

"He looks like I could blow him right over," I said.

Lena looked away from me, embarrassed. "He ain't young. Must be close to fifty now. His life ain't been easy."

"Yeah," I said, not buying it. "Whose has?"

"He wanted to come tonight. He says he wants to be a real daddy and do stuff with us. He tries. My daddy tries."

I rolled my eyes, then looked over at Dion.

"I keep her with me most times I can," Lena said. "It's safer that way."

"It's not fair," I said.

Sherry and a group of girls walked past us.

"Hey, WT. Hey, UT," Sherry said. The other girls in the group laughed. Someone called, "Good game, Marie," but I didn't catch who it was.

" 'Whitetrash' and 'Uncle Tom,' " I said to Lena.

"Figured that. You walking?"

"My dad's upstairs waiting for me. Probably flirting with some woman. You want to tell your father to go ahead home and drive with us?"

Lena shook her head. "He wouldn't like that. Got to go home with him. Maybe later on I'll try to sneak back out and walk some. It's pretty tonight, all those stars out everywhere."

"You're not going to hitch anywhere, are you?"

Lena smiled. "No."

"Swear?"

"Cross my heart."

"Well, I got to go shower before I melt the walls of this gym." I took a whiff of my underarm and grimaced. Lena laughed.

"Come on, Dion," she yelled.

Dion dropped the ball, then ran across the gym and slapped me on the backside. "That's how they do it?" she asked.

"Yeah!"

"Why everybody got to slap everybody's butts all the time?"

"It's the way," I said.

"Gross." Dion took Lena's hand. "We gonna come by for some more of that hot chocolate."

"Too much hot chocolate gives you worms," I said.

Dion raised her eyebrows. "You lie! You die!"

"You lie, *you* die," I said, gently shoving her head. "You know what?"

"What?" they asked in unison.

"You two have black-girl names."

"I don't got no black-girl name," Dion said, putting her hands on her hips.

"I don't got no black-girl name," I mimicked.

"Maybe we're light-skinned," Lena said.

Dion looked at the back of her hands. "We white, Lena," she said. "I thought we was white."

"I see you tomorrow." Lena laughed, dragging a panicked Dion out of the gym.

chapter **21**

A week before Thanksgiving break Lena began talking more about leaving. In the beginning I only half listened, figuring she was talking about the trips she took when her father messed with her. But after a while she became more persistent.

"Me and Dion, when we go, if I never see you again, I want you to know that I'm somewhere thinking about you, Marie."

Lena was sitting across from me at lunch, struggling to peel a half-ripe banana. She tried to sound casual. We were alone at our end of the lunch table. Sherry and her friends sat a couple of tables away. Every now and then Sherry glanced over in our direction, a longing in her eyes like I had never seen before. Some basketball buddies were sitting at the table next to ours. They were friendly enough, but I didn't feel like talking sports. Until Lena came, I hadn't realized how segregated things were at Chauncey. The swimming teams were all-white, both basketball teams were predominantly black, and the track team had all-black sprinters and all-white distance runners.

Right in the middle of me thinking about this, Lena's words sunk in.

"What are you talking about? Where are you gonna go in the middle of the school year?"

Lena shrugged and took a bite of her banana. I hated bananas and hated watching people eat them, so I looked away and bumped eyes with Sherry, who quickly turned back to her group.

"Just if," Lena said. "If anything ever happens and I don't get a chance to say good-bye or something . . ."

"What could happen?"

"I don't know," Lena said, her voice fading. "Just if. Just remember that, you know, you was important."

"Why are you saying this? Where the heck are you planning on going?"

Lena glanced around the cafeteria. "Remember my friend I told you about, the girl my daddy hated 'cause she was black?"

"Yeah?"

"I never got a chance to say good-bye to her. And my mama? I never got a chance to say good-bye to her neither."

I nodded. I wanted to reach across the table and touch Lena's shoulder, but I didn't. Maybe years and years from that moment I would regret it. I touched her hand.

Lena smiled knowingly. "Every morning when I drop Dion off, I give her a kiss and a hug 'cause you never know. . . ."

"You don't," I said, the image of Mama's back crossing my mind and fading.

"S'cuse me while I kiss the sky," Lena began singing softly. "S'cuse me while I kiss the sky."

I smiled. "Where'd you get that song from?"

"That's Jimi," Lena said as though I should have known. I must have looked pretty blank. "Jimi Hendrix, Marie."

"Yeah, I heard of him. Just didn't know what songs he did, that's all."

"Jimi was the best. I got a big poster of him, but my daddy don't let me put it up. Hey!" Lena stopped eating and lifted her schoolbag onto the table. "I got something for you."

"For *me*?"

"Yeah."

She handed me a flat package wrapped in a brown paper bag. I opened it slowly. It was a sketch of a line of weeping willows hanging over a lake underneath the bluest sky I'd ever seen. The lake seemed to reflect every single leaf and branch. The picture was all full of blues and greens and golds.

"It's beautiful," I said, holding the picture carefully, not wanting to mess it up with fingerprints. "Where'd you get it?"

"I *drew* it," Lena said. "Copped a box of color pencils from Woolworth's. They wanted four dollars for them! Get out of Dodge if you think I'm gonna pay four dollars for some cheapy colored pencils."

I looked at her.

"I ain't gonna steal no more," she said quickly. "Those pencils should last me a long time. Then I'll have some money maybe, to buy some."

"I didn't even know you drew," I said. "All this time and I didn't even know you could draw. This is so beautiful."

"Ain't nothing," Lena said, blushing. "You really like it?"

"I *love* it. It's just so . . . peaceful-looking."

"Peaceful," Lena repeated softly, leaning over the table to look at the picture with me. "Yeah, it is peaceful, ain't it? That how it make you feel? Peaceful?"

I nodded.

"Me too. When I'm drawing, it's like I go into another world or something. Nobody can't bother me. Guess that's why I draw those kinds of pictures all full of trees and water and sunshine. You think it's corny?"

"It's not corny. It's great. It's perfect."

"You think so, Marie? You think maybe I could be an artist or something if I wanted to?"

"The way you draw? No question!"

Lena looked off. "That's what I really want. More than anything, I think. I don't tell nobody, but that's what I really want. People might say I'm crazy thinking some girl like me could grow up to be an artist."

"You just have to keep trying, Lena. You just have to draw every single day on anything . . . anywhere."

Lena's eyes lit up. "That's what I do. Sometimes I draw on paper bags if I can't find paper. Sometimes I'm drawing in the bathroom and Dion's outside the door crying about how she gotta pee, but I don't let her in till I'm finished. I just keep on drawing and drawing."

"Kissing the sky," I said, staring at the picture.

"Huh?"

"That's what it makes me think about—that somebody's trying to kiss the sky."

Lena looked at the picture. "Kissing the sky . . . ," she said softly. "Like I'm kissing the sky."

"Any other lyrics besides that?" I asked.

Lena smiled, her eyes bright. "Yeah. But they ain't so important."

chapter **22**

Chauncey had its first Indian summer that year, and November temperatures shot up to seventy degrees. No one was prepared for the warm spell. We draped our coats over our heads or walked with them tied around our waists. When it was warm, Lena and I spent a lot of time in Randolph Park. It was a good distance from where either of us lived, but we had become walkers over the weeks, and I could feel the muscles in my thighs and calves flexing with every step. Lena moved quickly, her legs blasting out in front of her, her feet hitting the sidewalk hard. We must have looked like a strange pair walking the streets although in the one picture I have of us together (a picture some guy on the street shot with a Polaroid, then offered to us if we allowed him to take another—

Lena swore he took it home to jerk off to), I am surprised at how beautiful we look. In the shot the sun is almost down so that there is a gray and pink light behind us. Lena is looking directly into the camera, but I'm looking off so that only three quarters of my face is showing. But the guy taking the picture captured something—a look I had never really seen on either of our faces—a look that said neither of those girls in the picture trusts the world, but look how they're planning to blast through it. Lena is almost smiling in the picture, her eyes bright but skeptical. I'm not smiling at all, but my look isn't angry either. Our expressions say we've been interrupted, and as soon as this interruption is over, we'll move on.

By December the weather was back to normal, windy, cold, and snowy. Before old snow could melt, new snow was falling, and by mid-December Chauncey was layered in white.

Postcards continued to come from my mother from exotic islands lush and green as spring. But over time the postcards had begun to lose something. The islands seemed more unreal to me, had become places I'd never really want to go to. My mother became more unreal too. Her familiar handwriting on the back of the postcards was beginning to remind me of the letters we got from distant relatives. Maybe we'd see them again soon. Maybe we wouldn't. Either way life would go on. My father's divorce papers finally came through, and he began to talk more and more about the women he'd met at work and at the clubs he sometimes went to with friends.

"Maybe I'll go on a date sometime," he said as though he was testing me, to see if I was ready for this news. We were sitting on the sunporch Daddy had encased with storm glass, drinking hot chocolate. It was bright outside, the sun reflecting off the snow.

"That would be nice," I said, really meaning it.

"Yeah," my father said, looking out into the yard and smiling, a light behind his eyes I hadn't seen in a long time. "It would be."

The place around where my mother once was had begun closing over, a dull scar of a memory taking the place of what had once been an out-and-out longing to have her back in our lives.

"What does it feel like?" I asked Lena one Sunday. "After somebody you love dies?"

"You wake up one morning and realize it's the first morning in a long time that you ain't woke up crying. Then the next morning maybe you cry again. Then the next maybe you don't. That's how it goes. A little bit at a time until you're all right."

"Is it ever all gone away?" I asked. "I mean, does it ever feel *all* right?"

Lena shook her head. "Not that I know of. But my life ain't over yet."

Sitting on the sunporch with Daddy now, we didn't know if we'd wake up crying for Mama tomorrow. But that morning the sun was streaming in and hot chocolate warmed our stomachs. That morning we were all right.

chapter **23**

Lena and I were not in the "bright group." Our grades seemed to ebb and flow. One week I'd get a ninety on an English test, the next week I'd fail. One week Lena would ace her math quiz, the following week she'd get a D on a social studies paper.

"If you'd sit down and study sometime instead of running around with that Lena girl," my father scolded when he saw my first-trimester report card, "you can do better than this." He shook the card disgustedly, signed it, and handed it back to me. "I don't know what makes you think you'll get into a good college with grades like this."

I rolled my eyes and looked off. My father got full tuition remission at Ohio University. We both knew this was where I'd end up as long as I did okay.

But it was different for Lena.

"If I don't do better, I ain't gonna be no artist," she said. "I won't be nowhere."

"Yeah," I said.

We were leaning against the fence that encased the big swings in Randolph Park. The park was nearly empty.

"It don't matter." Lena took a pen from her back pocket to sign her report card. "What's the chances some college is gonna want me?"

"You could get a scholarship. If you worked, just studied a little more."

Lena frowned. "I can't keep my mind in one place. It goes off and does what it feels like."

"But you could learn, Lena." I didn't realize I was pleading with her until I heard my own voice. She sounded so hopeless—as though everything in the world that was good had to happen to another person. I remembered that look in her eyes the first day I met her, the one that took over when Sherry called her whitetrash. "You could try really hard," I said even though I realized then that Lena had lost hope a long time ago.

For the first time I began to understand the privilege I had. My father was a college professor. I never had to worry about money or the future. There was money waiting for me when I turned twenty-one. I had no idea how much, but my father had assured me it would be enough to help me

95

glide easily through the rest of my life. My clothes were expensive. My father had a thing about well-made stuff and wouldn't let me buy anything that wasn't made from natural fibers. I looked over at Lena. She was wearing a beat-up-looking sweatshirt and dingy jeans. The clothes looked as though they had never been new. And my daddy loved me. No matter what else. He was a good man and he loved me.

"What you looking at?" Lena asked, checking herself.

"You want some of my clothes?"

Lena narrowed her eyes. "What I want your clothes for?"

I shrugged. "I could give you an outfit." I pictured the walk-in closet Daddy had built for me and the rows of jeans, shirts, jackets, and skirts hanging neatly from one end to the other. Rows of shoes and sneakers were lined up underneath.

"I got my own clothes," Lena said. "I don't need your stupid stuff."

The air went out of me like someone punching me in the stomach. I stared up at the bare trees, trying to force my tears back. My stuff wasn't stupid. Why did I feel so stupid?

"Hey," Lena said after a moment, touching my shoulder. "Marie."

I turned back. She tossed her head and pulled a cigarette from her pocket, lowering her eyes to stare at the flame as she lit it.

"I ain't mean it, Marie." Lena let go of some smoke, blowing it out of the side of her mouth. "I just don't need no give-aways, okay?"

I shrugged, and rolled my eyes. Maybe she saw how hurt I was.

"The world goes like this, don't it?" Lena said, moving the hand holding the cigarette through the air like a roller coaster.

"Yeah," I said. "Whatever."

Lena went on as though I hadn't spoken. "My family's at a low point right now. Ain't got the extra quarter to call for help. But it won't always be like this. One day up. One day down. Happens to everybody."

"If you didn't want the clothes, all you had to say was no. You didn't have to say they were stupid."

"Said I was sorry. You know I ain't mean it that way."

I *did* know, but I was just mad. Mad at the world.

"Look at that child," Lena said, pointing. In the distance Dion was slowly making her way toward us, trailing a tree branch, her coat open and flapping against her arms.

"Button your coat up, girl," Lena yelled. She shook her head. "She don't have the sense she was born with."

The coat was too big for Dion, while Lena's coat was on the small side. But the coats were heavy enough to keep the chill out. Maybe that was all they needed.

chapter

Postcard from my mother. Phoenix, Arizona.

> The sky here burns bright orange, withers to black
> then, somebody or is it something?
> is gone.

> Love, Me

Love me. I sat at the kitchen table staring at the card. Was she asking us to love her, even though? Did she think we didn't anymore? The cards, with their tiny half-note, half-poem messages, had never been enough. In the beginning I had been frustrated, reading each one over and over again with the hopes of getting something more from them. But there were no real messages between the lines, at least nothing I could decipher. Now I had begun to take each message as literally as I possibly could. Still there were questions that needed answering. Was she happy? Did she still have to take her medicine? Did she miss me so much it hurt? What would she say about Lena?

I stared out the window. The night before, it had snowed, and now the sun was shining brightly, melting the snow into thin rivers that ran down the stairs on this side of the house. Strips of yellow sunlight shone across the table. Turning from the window, I watched the dust-encased streams of light move about, without direction.

The doorbell rang. I waited for Daddy to answer it, then remembered it was Saturday and he was on a date with Rose, the town librarian.

"It's us," I heard Dion calling. "Open up. It's freezing out here."

"It's your fault, Marie," Lena said as they rushed in. "You're the one who introduced her to Mr. Bubble."

"I'm gonna stay in the tub for a whole hour," Dion said, running ahead of us.

"Scrub your ears," Lena called as Dion disappeared up the stairs and down the hall toward my bathroom.

"Put your stuff in my room," I yelled.

I heard the bathroom door slam.

"She's gonna use too much of that stuff and start itching," Lena said, shucking her coat and following me into the kitchen.

I shook my head. "Not that much left."

"She better save me some, then."

"I got another one," I said, handing her my mother's postcard.

Lena looked at the picture before turning the card over. "Who wants to be in Arizona! All they got out there is air!"

"Hot air," I said. "I checked the temperature in the paper. It's going up to ninety-seven there."

Lena raised her eyebrows. "Shoot. Wish we was there."

Dion had brought her pajamas with her. Half an hour later she padded down the stairs in them. "I didn't leave no ring," she said, settling down two inches from the television.

"Not so close," Lena said. Dion moved back a half inch and used the remote to flip through Saturday-morning cartoons. "Where's your pops?"

I brought Dion a cup of hot chocolate. "He's out on a date," I said, following Lena upstairs.

Dion turned and rolled her eyes. "That's so corny," she said.

"You can come in now," Lena called. When I entered, she was up to her neck in bubbles. The bathroom was steamy and smelled of soap. Lena smiled, holding up a handful of bubbles.

I sat on the toilet. "You want me to keep reading this?" I held up *The Cancer Journals* by Audre Lorde. It was one of the few books my mother left behind, and I knew the only reason she left it was because she had two copies. I had slipped this one out of the box of books my father had packed to send to the Salvation Army. "It's like looking into some-body's diary," Lena said the first time I read from it. It was the story of Audre Lorde's battle with breast cancer.

"That don't make me sad about my mama's cancer," Lena had said. "Just makes me wish I had swiped it from a bookstore when she was still living."

Now Lena nodded, sank deeper into the tub, and closed her eyes. Lena didn't have anything remotely resembling breasts yet, and mine were too small to give a second thought to. But we were both way into *The Cancer Journals.* "It's like we're getting ready for something," Lena always said. Only neither of us knew exactly what that some-thing was.

" 'I have found,' " I read softly, " 'that battling despair does not mean closing my eyes to the enormity of the tasks of effecting change, nor ignoring the strength and the bar-barity of the forces aligned against us. It means teaching, sur-viving and fighting with the most important resource I have, myself, and taking joy in that battle. It means, for me, recognizing the enemy outside and the enemy within, and knowing that my work is part of a continuum of women's work, of reclaiming this earth and our power, and knowing that this work did not begin with my birth nor will it end with my death, . . .' "

"What work?" Lena asked, opening one eye.

"I guess . . . living," I said.

"Oh. Keep reading."

" '. . . And it means knowing that within this continuum, my life and my love and my work has particular power and meaning relative to others.

" 'It means trout fishing on the Missisquoi River at dawn and tasting the green silence, and knowing that this beauty too is mine forever.' "

I stopped reading and stared out the window above Lena's head. Was my mother fishing on the Missisquoi?

"Where is the Missisquoi, Marie?"

"I don't know."

"And green silence. You think it taste sweet?"

"Probably."

Lena sighed. "I want to fish the Missisquoi and taste sweet, green silence."

"Me too."

chapter **25**

Lena began to change. At school she walked quickly, hurry-ing from class to class, not waiting for me.

"I can't be late," she said when I caught up to her.

"Why not? You've never cared about being late before."

"I just can't. Not no more."

One Saturday went by without her and Dion showing up for their baths. Then another.

"You ever coming back to my house on Saturdays?" I asked on the second Monday.

"You saying I smell?" Lena shot back, her eyes hard and dark.

I must have looked hurt because she hugged me quickly, then smiled. "I got stuff I gotta do now, Marie."

"Like what?"

"I gotta figure out how me and Dion can taste that sweet, green silence before it's too late."

I nodded. "Randolph Park," I said quickly. "When Dion's sliding across the ice and we're talking. Let's go today—"

"Really taste it, Marie." Lena took my hand and pressed her thumb into my palm.

"Don't go anywhere, Lena," I said suddenly. "Don't ever."

Lena pressed her finger to her lips. She looked at me, then blinked and shook her head.

We walked to our next class, our fingers fiercely intertwined.

At lunch that day Sherry walked up to our table. Lena and I were sitting poring over some notes before Lena's English class. Maybe if she got better grades, she'd stay and stop thinking about the sweet, green silence. Lena's head was so close to the book, her nose almost touched the page.

"Hey," Sherry said, sitting down next to me, her milk straw sticking out from the side of her mouth. She had gotten her hair cut almost as short as mine, way shorter than Lena's, which had grown past her ears over the months.

"Hey, yourself," I said.

Lena looked up from her book.

"Hey," Sherry said. They looked at each other for a long

time until Lena kind of smiled out of the side of her mouth and Sherry smiled back. I had missed Sherry.

"Hey, yourself," Lena said. "What you know good?"

Sherry shifted the straw from one side of her mouth to the other. "No thing but a chicken wing," she said.

I couldn't help thinking of this beautiful scene: me and Sherry and Lena walking in the park hand in hand in hand, laughing like something out of a Martin Luther King, Jr., dream, where he hoped one day little black girls and little white girls joined hands. *Yeah,* I was thinking, *it could happen like this.*

chapter 26

"There's a way two people remain friends forever and ever, Marie," Lena said. We were sitting on the big swings, swinging slowly, lazily dragging our feet back and forth against the tarp. The sun broke through the clouds in bright splinters. Lena was wearing a dungaree jacket, long black skirt, and black Dr. Martens boots tied with red and black laces. She looked nice. I didn't ask where she got the clothes.

"How?" I asked, although I didn't really feel like talking. The park was empty, and it felt good just to sit with Lena in the silence.

"Secrets," Lena said.

"What about them?"

Lena kicked back and let herself swing hard, then just as quickly dragged her boots to stop herself.

"You keep them."

"I do keep them."

"Will you keep the secret about my father?"

I nodded. "I said I would, right?"

"But will you?"

"Of course."

"Now I need a secret from you, though. Something you've never told anyone and probably never will."

"I write my mother," I said. "I tell her everything."

Lena looked at me and frowned. "I thought you didn't have an address for her."

"I don't. I don't send the letters anywhere. They're all in a box in the back of my closet."

"Oh." Lena was silent.

"She's not coming back. I know it."

"Yeah," Lena said. "I know it too."

"It's okay, though, I think. Writing her those letters, it's a way of getting her out of my system but at the same time . . . keeping her close to me."

"But telling her is like telling nobody . . . ," Lena said.

"But at the same time telling someone."

I held my hand out and waited for Lena to clutch it. Then we started swinging high enough to feel like if we wanted to, if we jumped out into the sky, maybe we could fly.

chapter **27**

Lena began missing school. I walked by her house, afraid to go in. Tiny kids were playing in the graveled parking lot surrounding it. I watched them for a moment, thinking of asking one of them to go get Lena. But then I thought, *What if her father is home?* I blinked, and the house blurred. What if things were going on?

Without thinking, I headed up the parking lot and knocked hard on the door Lena had pointed out to me months before.

"Who is it?" I heard Dion call.

"It's Marie. Where's Lena?"

Dion came to the door in dirty pajamas and stood with her tiny body blocking my entrance. I smelled something strong, like cats, drift past her. Behind her the room was gray and dusty-looking.

"Hi," Dion said. Crumbs dotted the side of her mouth, and she had a tiny milk mustache. It was close to dinnertime.

"Hi," I said. "Lena around?" I tried to sound casual.

"Nope," Dion said. "She went out with Daddy."

I felt relieved, then scared all over again.

"Who's babysitting you, then?"

"My *own* self." Dion raised her eyebrows and looked at me as though I had just asked the world's dumbest question.

I looked around nervously. "Tell Lena to call me," I said. "Tell her I came by."

Dion nodded, then shut the door. Walking away, I glanced through the window and saw Dion sitting in front of the television.

At home that night I stayed close to the phone, trying not to seem as though I was waiting. Daddy came in at seven, ate the spaghetti and sausage I'd made for dinner, then showered and began dressing for a date.

"What do you think of this?" he asked nervously, coming to the top of the stairs. I looked up from my magazine and checked out his shirt and pants.

"You look nice," I said. He had shaved and combed his hair back with oil so that it glistened.

"You really think so?"

I smiled. He sounded like a little boy.

"You look absolutely great, Daddy," I said.

He grinned as he came down the stairs.

"We're just going out for dessert and coffee," he said, stopping at the door and blowing me a kiss. "You be good."

"No, *you* be good," I teased, blowing a kiss back to him. "You be *real* good."

He raised an eyebrow at me. "Uh-oh. Teenage daughter talking," he said. "Big, big uh-oh."

"Don't worry, Daddy. I'll only be a teenager for another seven years. Then the worst part of your life will be over."

The phone rang just as Daddy's car pulled away. I picked it up before it could ring again.

"Hey, Marie," Lena said. Her voice sounded as though there were miles and miles and miles between us.

"Where are you?" I nearly yelled into the phone. "Did Dion tell you I went by your house?"

Lena laughed, but it wasn't a funny laugh. "Yeah. I was out with my father."

"Where?"

Lena laughed again, and I remembered her telling me about nerves—how she laughed sometimes because of her nerves, even when nothing was funny.

"What's going on, Lena?" I felt sick. Something was wrong. *Really* wrong.

"He's touching Dion now," Lena said. "I told him touch me but please don't touch Dion." Lena was laughing so hard,

I could barely understand her. "But he just cursed me. I gotta take care of me and Dion, Marie. I gotta."

"I'm calling the cops," I said. "I'm telling them—"

"Don't!" Lena breathed heavily and hiccuped. " 'Cause we leaving here, Marie. Me and Dion leaving."

"Maybe there's a way you can stay if I call the cops. . . ."

"We leaving, Marie. I just wanted to tell you. When we get to where we're going, I'll write you. I swear."

"Don't go, Lena," I cried. "We could tell somebody. Please don't go."

"I'll write you, Marie." Then the phone went dead.

I stood there for a long time until a recording came on to announce the phone was off the hook. I stared at the receiver. I wanted my mother. More than anything in the world.

chapter **28**

Every day I walk past a FOR RENT sign in the window of the house where Lena and Dion once lived. I know the way the white letters of the sign curve against their red background. I know that the fourth pane in the window has a crack running diagonally across it. I know if you press your face against the glass, you can see inside. There are dustballs flying around in there. In one corner a broom sits upside down, its bristles brushing against the gray-blue wall. A naked lightbulb hangs from the ceiling. A piece of paper with a tiny bit of a picture drawn on it is lying right in the center of the floor. Outside the front door I found a piece of notebook paper with their names written on it in Lena's handwriting: *Elena Cecilia Bright and her sister Edion Kay Bright lived here once.* I had to swallow when I came across Dion's name. I had never known it. What other things about them hadn't I known? Had Lena left this piece of paper hoping one day I'd find it? Will she ever know that it's laminated now, in a corner of my drawer where I can look at it whenever I want and remember them?

Each morning I expect to see their grainy faces on a milk carton. Sad, hard faces looking out at the world, daring it to say something about them leaving.

Each morning my father comes into my room and, taking my face between his hands, asks if I'm okay. His hands are warm and softer than the hands I remembered. In the beginning, when I leaned into him to cry, those hands were awkward but gentle as they patted the back of my head. "Go ahead, Marie," Daddy whispered. "It's okay to cry." As though he were saying it was okay to cry for everyone who has left my life.

But now, when my father takes my face into his hands and searches my eyes, he doesn't understand why the tears have been replaced with something unbreakable. A sweet, green silence that is screaming inside of me, *Yes! Yes! They got away!* I am waiting, though, giving them time to get distance.

I imagine Dion walking beside Lena, her hand inside of Lena's, her small sneaker kicking at a rock. I imagine them walking through the beautiful places in the world, together.

Sometimes I feel Lena at the edge of my shoulder, her breath smoky and warm. Sometimes the empty seat in homeroom is filled with the ghostly presence of her, and I hear the crackling of a cupcake wrapper.

A postcard from my mother said, "You never wake up any morning sure of your life's interaction with the day." Before I leave the house, I write her a note, "No, Mama, you don't. But so what? You get through it, if you're strong enough—and move on!" then crawl to the back of my closet to add it to the stack of letters there.

A cold wind blows up suddenly as I turn the corner by Woolworth's. I open and close my mouth like a fish, lifting my head to catch big gulps of air against the back of my throat, not caring that people are looking. Dion and Lena. Two girls on a walkabout. I smile, fighting back tears, suddenly feeling a hundred years older than everyone. *I'm only twelve,* I want to shout. Instead I turn and head toward Sherry's house, knowing that in three weeks it could be like Lena never was. The world puts us here for the quickest second, then snatches us right back up again.

We all just people here, I hear Lena say.

"Yes," I whisper, reaching to ring Sherry's bell. "Why can't we all just be people here?"